Conker
and
Nudge

Adria Meserve

Piccadilly Press • London

There once were two anteaters
called Conker and Nudge.

Conker was the big one with
the long nose and the bushy tail.
Nudge was his little brother.

Nudge adored his big brother.

He wanted to do
everything Conker did.

"I want to juggle ants . . .

build the tallest towers . . .

and swing on vines," he told Conker.

"Just like you."

Sometimes Conker liked being
a big brother and would
help Nudge.

"Look and learn,"
he told him,
"and one day you
could be clever,
strong and
brave like me."

Sometimes Conker found his little brother VERY annoying.

"Don't be such a silly snout!" he said when he was showing Nudge how to swing through the trees and Nudge still got things wrong.

One day Conker was practising his balancing act. Nudge wanted to balance too, but he kept getting in the way.

"Watch out, Clumsy Claws!" Conker said. "You'll make me fall!"

They ended up in a tangled heap on the ground.

"STOP COPYING ME!"
shouted Conker.

"Go away! I'm going to play with my friends."

"Let's go somewhere Nudge would be too scared to follow,"
said Conker to Capybara and Armadillo.
"I know!" he said. "Let's go on
a Giant Ant Hunt."

"Can I come?"
Nudge asked.

"No! You're too small,"
Conker said.

Conker and his friends SKIPPED and HOPPED
across a slippery log . . .

They HACKED their way
through the thick puckerbrush . . .

They RAFTED down a raging river . . .

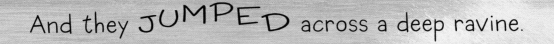

And they JUMPED across a deep ravine.

"We are clever,
we are strong and
we are very brave!"
Conker sang.

They had just reached
the most delicious-looking
giant anthill, when they
heard a rustling sound.
"Ssshhh," whispered Conker.
"What's that?"

"LOOK OUT!" cried Nudge.

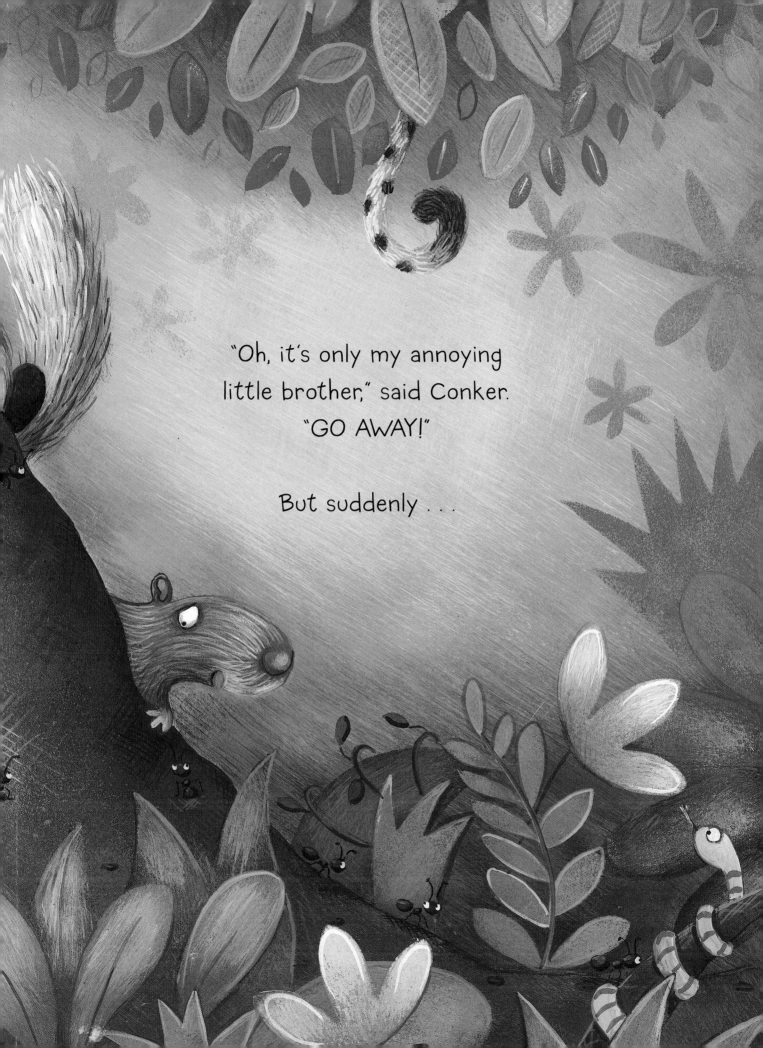

"Oh, it's only my annoying
little brother," said Conker.
"GO AWAY!"

But suddenly . . .

ROAR!

A jaguar jumped out at them!

Capybara fled
down a hole in
the ground.

Armadillo curled up in a ball and hid in his armoured shell.

But Conker couldn't find anywhere to hide. "Oh no! My nose is too long and my tail is too big. I don't know what to do!"

HELP!

At that moment, someone came
swinging fast through the trees . . .
It was NUDGE!

"Quick,
Conker!
Jump on!"
he shouted.

And they swung to safety.

"You are the bravest brother in
the world," said Conker
and gave Nudge a big hug.
"How did you learn to
swing on a vine like that?"
"By copying you, like
I always do," said Nudge.

On the way home, Conker helped Nudge
jump across the ravine . . .

and showed him how to hack through
the puckerbush with his tail.

When Nudge was too tired to walk,
Conker carried him home.

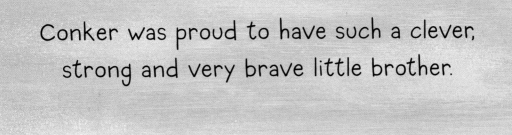

Conker was proud to have such a clever,
strong and very brave little brother.

And after that, Conker let Nudge join
in when he played with his friends . . .
Well, *sometimes!*

For Pedro and Quique, with love

First published in Great Britain in 2008 by
Piccadilly Press Ltd, 5 Castle Road, London NW1 8PR
www.piccadillypress.co.uk

Text and illustration copyright © Adria Meserve, 2008

Designed by Simon Davis
Printed and bound in China by WKT
Colour reproduction by Dot Gradations

ISBN: 978 1 85340 959 2 (paperback)
978 1 85340 960 8 (hardback)

1 3 5 7 9 10 8 6 4 2